Big Book of Fun

CREDITS

Pages 6-7 | POGO PIRATES!
Based on the book *Let's Get Jumping!*, written by Melinda La Rose, illustrated by Alan Batson

Page 34-35 | SAVING THE GAME
Based on the book *Squeeze in a Pinch*, written by Susan Amerikaner, illustrated by Alan Batson

Page 40-41 | THE CIRCUS STAR
Based on the book *The Circus Comes to Town*, written by Melinda La Rose, illustrated by Alan Batson

Page 44-45 | DAY TRIP FUN
Based on the book *Road Trip*, written by Lori C. Froeb, illustrated by Loter, Inc.

Page 65-71 | A VERY LOUD FRIEND
Based on the episode written by Noelle Wright
Based on the book *Loud Louie*
Story concept by Sheila Sweeny Higginson, illustrated by Alan Batson

Page 74-75 | A NEW ARRIVAL
Based on the book *Jake Hatches a Plan*, written by Melinda La Rose, illustrated by Alan Batson

Page 97-103 | A TIRED RACECAR
Based on the episode written by Kurt Redeker
Written by Sheila Sweeny Higginson, illustrated by Alan Batson

Page 107-111 | THE COLORS OF THE RAINBOW
Based on the book *Minnie's Rainbow*, written by Sheila Sweeny Higginson
Story concept by Tea Orsi, illustrated by Loter, Inc.

Page 130-131 | A GREAT NOSE
Written by Catherine Such

Page 134-135 | SHARING THE SLIDE
Written by Catherine Such

Page 138-139 | SOFIA'S DANCE LESSON
Based on the book *Sofia the First*, written by Catherine Hapka, illustrated by Grace Lee

Page 140-141 | FIXING FEET
Based on the episode written by Mike Rabb
Based on the book *Cowboy Manny*, written by Susan Ring, illustrated by Alan Batson

Page 164-165 | A BRIGHT NIGHT
Based on the book *A Very Handy Holiday*, written by Susan Ring, illustrated by Alan Batson

This edition published by Parragon Books Ltd in 2014
and distributed by

Parragon Inc.
440 Park Avenue South, 13th Floor
New York, NY 10016
www.parragon.com

ISBN 978-1-4723-6404-3

Printed in China

Big Book of Fun

Parragon

Bath • New York • Cologne • Melbourne • Delhi
Hong Kong • Shenzhen • Singapore • Amsterdam

POGO PIRATES!

1

2

Jake and the crew were having fun,
They were playing without a care.
When a wooden box washed ashore,
Jake said, "I wonder what's in there?"

Jake carefully opened the box,
And let out a big shout.
"It's a POGO STICK!" he cried,
"Quick, let's take it out!"

3

4

Cubby tried out the POGO STICK,
"It's wobbly!" he said with a sigh.
Nobody noticed Captain Hook,
Spying on them from nearby.

Hook wanted the POGO STICK,
And he had a sneaky plan.
He used his plunger to grab it,
Then shouted, "Catch me if you can!"

? Can you SPOT these details in the pictures?

6

5

Hook jumped onto the POGO STICK,
And bounced off as fast as he could.
But he soon lost control,
His pogoing wasn't very good!

6

Before he knew what happened,
Hook had bounced into a tree!
"I'm stuck!" he shouted loudly,
"Somebody come rescue me!"

7

Luckily Izzy was nearby,
"I'll rescue you if I must!"
She quickly flew up the tree,
And sprinkled him with pixie dust.

8

With the POGO STICK safely back,
Cubby had another try.
"I'm much better than Hook!"
He laughed as he bounced by!

7

Starting School

Answers on page 171

? Sofia is going to start classes at Royal Prep. She will meet her teachers and classmates—what a thrill! But first she's got to pack her schoolbag. CHECK the things she needs.

8

DANCE MOVES

Sofia is learning how to dance, but it takes lots of practice. To give her a hand, NUMBER the dancing sequence. A little hint? Start with a royal curtsy!

Answer on page 171

Doc's Drawings

?

What do different animals look like? Doc's drawn pictures to show her friends. Which crayons has she used? MATCH the five animals on her poster with the right color crayons. Hint: three of the colors shown below are not used.

SPOT the pencil holder hidden in the scene!

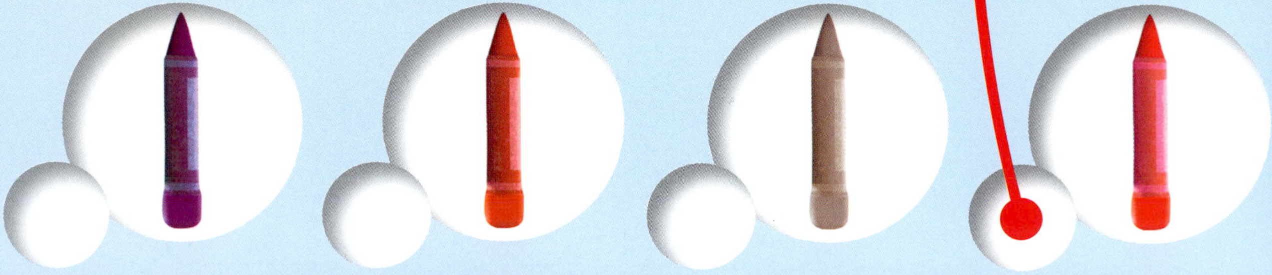

10

Answers on page 171

11

BUILD A RACER

It's fun to MAKE your own racer, to race with friends. Mickey thinks so, too! FOLLOW the four easy steps and take off at full speed!

ASK an adult to HELP you.

1 You'll need: paper tube; black card stock; safety scissors; stickers; cotton swabs; acrylic paint; paintbrush.

2 Cut the paper tube in half. Paint each half and then cut out four wheels from the black card stock.

3 Insert two cotton swabs into each paper tube and push the card stock wheels onto the ends.

4 Draw race numbers and drivers on the stickers and apply them to the tubes. VROOM, let's go!

GO

START

13

BEACH VOLLEYBALL!

?

Jake and Izzy are great beach volleyball players. They've just scored their first point against Hook and Bones! Would you like to see a replay? FOLLOW the dotted lines with a pencil, from number one through to four, to COMPLETE the sequence of shots. Then ORDER the four balls below, from the smallest to the biggest.

1   3

1

Answer on page 171

PARTY TIME

? Today these families are having a block party. Oso's mission? To help out with the decorations! SPOT the five differences in the second picture.

16

GREEN FINGERS!

? Oso knows how nice it is to live in a green world, so he explains to his friend how to plant flowers. She will need at least three things! CHECK the objects that Oso uses to plant flowers in the backyard.

1 2 3

Brilliant Balloons!

?

Goofy is entertaining his friends with colorful balloon sculptures. Look at all of the different shapes! MATCH each balloon in the scene with the right shape in the panel.

TRACE the balloon Goofy's holding and COLOR it.

18

Answers on page 171

OUT TO SEA

? These dolphins have invited Jake and the crew out to sea for some fun! Which floating vehicles can they take? CHECK the ones they can use, then COLOR in the two white dolphins.

ONE CUPCAKE FACH

Answers on page 171

Doc has invited her friends over for tea and cupcakes. FOLLOW the paths to see whose cupcake is whose. Then COLOR them in.

22

HELICOPTER RESCUE

? Poor little helicopter! It crashed into a tree and is broken. But Doc's here to fix it. Now the helicopter is as good as new. Put these three scenes in the right ORDER.

Answer on page 171

CIRCUS ACTS!

?

Three cheers for the performers! Today our Clubhouse friends have decided to show off their many talents. TRACE the paths of the circus props in motion.

POOR HAND

? Doc's little brother Donny is playing with Alma and her Huggy Monkey Dolls. One of them has hurt its hand. But Doc soon fixes it, and everyone can get back to playing again. Put these three scenes in the right ORDER!

26

Answer on page 171

A Carriage for Sofia

?

Classes have finished at Royal Prep, and now it's time to go home by carriage. Sofia sees hers and recognizes every detail! SPOT the three shown below and CHECK them.

Answers on page 171

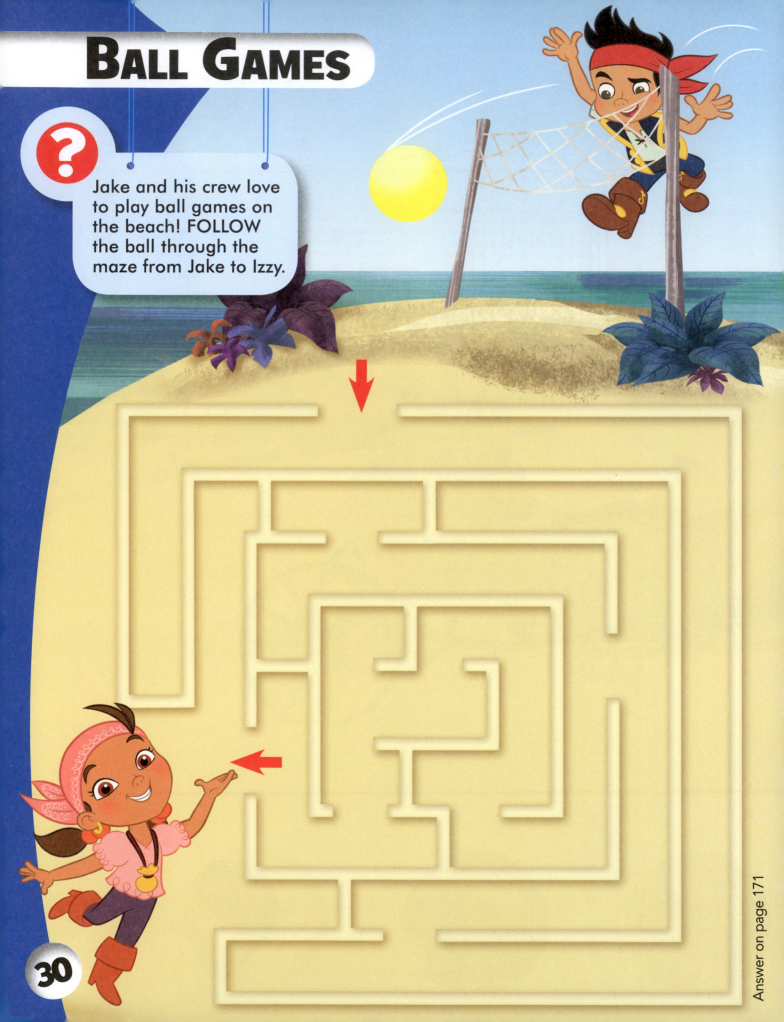

BALL GAMES

Jake and his crew love to play ball games on the beach! FOLLOW the ball through the maze from Jake to Izzy.

Answer on page 171

30

SHADOW SHAPES

? Have fun making shadow shapes with your hands! Which animal's shadow has Cubby made? CHECK the right animal below.

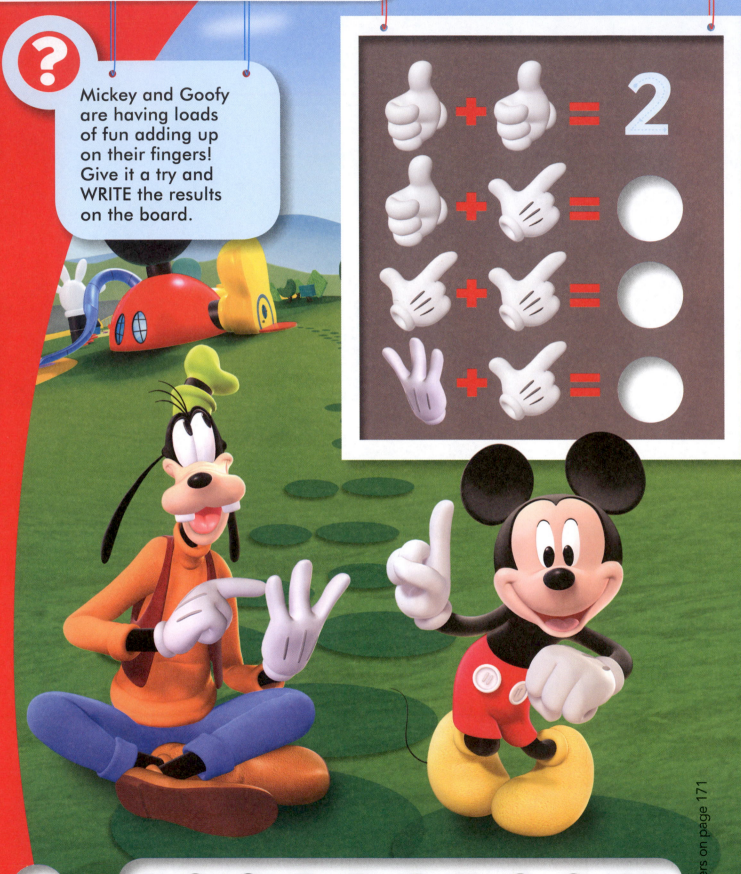

COUNTING FUN!

? Mickey and Goofy are having loads of fun adding up on their fingers! Give it a try and WRITE the results on the board.

1 2 3 4 5 6 7 8 9 10

Answers on page 171

TRAIN PICS!

?

Minnie and Daisy love taking pictures and printing them for their albums, like these ones of the Clubhouse gang on the train. SPOT the five differences in the second picture!

Answers on page 171

SAVING THE GAME

1

Down at the baseball field,
The Tools had a job to do.
Some broken seats needed fixing,
Before the game began at two.

2

Everyone quickly got to work,
Manny knew what had to be done.
He asked Squeeze to pull out a bolt,
Squeeze cried, "This will be fun!"

OUCH! MY THUMB!

3

But Squeeze missed the bolt,
And caught hold of Manny's THUMB!
Manny cried out, "Ouch!"
And then his THUMB went numb!

4

Poor Squeeze felt terrible,
"Your THUMB looks like a balloon!"
"Don't worry," Manny told her,
"It'll be okay again soon."

 What is the right ball to play baseball? CHECK it!

5

Later, Squeeze still felt bad.
A tear fell from her eye.
"My THUMB is feeling better,
Don't worry, please don't cry."

6

"Everybody makes mistakes,"
Manny told his friend.
"Don't give up, just try again,
It will work out in the end."

7

So Squeeze had another try,
And pulled the bolt right out.
"Well done, now let's fix the seats!"
Said Manny with a shout.

8

Later, the home team won the game,
The Tools cheered from the side.
The coach said it was thanks to them,
"Hooray for Team Tools!" he cried.

Answer on page 171

EYES AND EARS

? Doc's taking a good look at her stereo because the CD won't turn! MATCH the missing parts to the picture. Then TRACE the word to find out what Doc and the toys would like to listen to.

MUSIC

THE SWIM IS ON!

?

Jake and Izzy have challenged Hook and Smee to a swimming race. You and a friend can join them in this splashing competition! Take turns to ROLL the die and MOVE that number of spaces. Watch out for the objects floating along in the water—you must FOLLOW the instructions in the box if you land on them!

14

15

13

12

11

10

START

38

1

2

Time to relax?
LOSE 1 TURN!

+ 2

Nothing can stop you!
GO FORWARD 2 SPACES!

-2

Still learning to swim!
GO BACK 2 SPACES!

FINISH

16 · 17 · 18

9 · 8 · 7 · 6

3 · 4 · 5

THE CIRCUS STAR

1

You're all inside the TENT!

2

Miss Jolly was very busy,
She was planning a circus show.
She saw Ellyvan outside the TENT,
And asked him to have a go.

As he looked inside the circus TENT,
Ellyvan wondered what he could do.
Everyone was practicing hard,
Zooter said, "We'll find an act for you."

3

4

"Try the trapeze," suggested Zooter,
"You need to be nice and strong."
But Ellyvan was far too heavy,
He didn't stay in the air for long!

Next Ellyvan tried the see-saw,
The Beetle Bugs sat on the other side.
But the see-saw didn't move at all,
"I'm too heavy!" Ellyvan cried.

? Can you SPOT these details in the pictures?

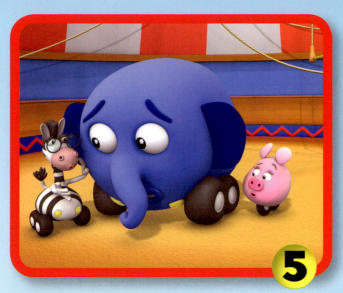

5

Ellyvan had run out of ideas,
He was feeling rather blue.
"I'm just too big for the circus,
There's nothing for me to do."

6

Suddenly there was a crash,
Miss Jolly had a big frown.
Taxicrab had hit the TENT pole,
And the TENT was falling down!

7

Quickly Ellyvan held the TENT up,
He knew what he had to do.
"You've saved the day!" said Miss Jolly,
"And found your circus act, too!"

8

Later on, at the circus show,
Miss Jolly introduced a special guest.
"It's Ellyvan, the strongest elephant,
In Jungle Junction he's the best!"

41

THE WAITING ROOM

Patients come and go in Doc's clinic. A nice glass of water is just what they need while they wait for a checkup! SPOT the five differences in the second picture.

Answers on page 171

42

A Mystery Dish

?

Today Doc is in the kitchen, helping to wash ingredients for a healthy meal. She's trying to guess what her mom is making for dinner. To find out, TRACE the first word below, then CROSS OUT each letter A in the next line and COPY the letters that are left into the second box.

VEGETABLE

S A̶ O A̶ U P

S _ _ _ _

Answer on page 171

DAY TRIP FUN

1

The Clubhouse friends were very busy
Packing food for a trip away.
They were off to the beach
To have a fun-filled day.

2

The sandwiches were packed.
"They look yummy!" Daisy cried.
"We're nearly ready to go,
So let's take everything outside."

3

While our friends loaded up the CAR,
Mickey noticed something wrong.
"The CAR has a flat tire,
I'll fix it before too long."

THE CAR IS FIXED!

4

Soon the CAR was good as new.
"Right!" said Mickey with a shout.
"Everybody find a seat,
Get ready for a fun day out!"

? A picnic on the beach? CHECK the wrong object!

5

But the CAR took a wrong turn!
"Oh dear!" Goofy said.
Luckily Mickey had a map.
"Let's take this road instead."

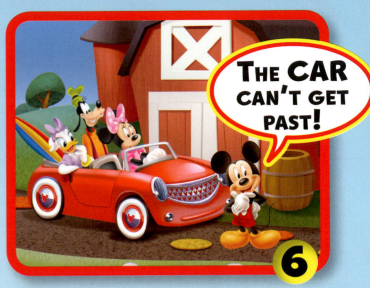

THE CAR CAN'T GET PAST!

6

The friends reached a farm at last,
But something was blocking the way.
They had to stop the CAR because
There was a horse, eating hay!

7

It was a very stubborn horse,
And it didn't want to play!
"Don't worry!" said Donald bravely,
"I can move it out of the way!"

8

When at last they reached the beach,
Mickey said, "Our journey's done!
It took a long time to get here,
But now it's time for lots of fun!"

45

Answer on page 171

Sky Scenes

? Jake is telling Cubby about how the sky changes throughout the day. At dawn it's yellow and orange, then it's blue when the sun is high, and when night falls the moon comes out. Put these three scenes in the right ORDER!

46

Answer on page 171

RAINBOW COLORS!

Izzy and Jake have spotted a rainbow in the sky! Help them CHECK the seven colors of the rainbow below. Hint: two of the colors below are not in the rainbow.

Answers on page 171

DIS-OVERING NATURE

? Doc is learning how to plant flowers, with her dad's help. MATCH the missing parts to the picture.

Answers on page 171

RONDA'S CHECKUP

? Uh-oh, Ronda's got spots on her skin—could it be chickenpox? No! She's been playing near the flowers, and now she's got a rash! SPOT the 5 differences in the second picture.

49

Answers on page 171

SPOTLIGHT ON WORDS!

Mickey's photos are in a mess! Match each picture with the right word.

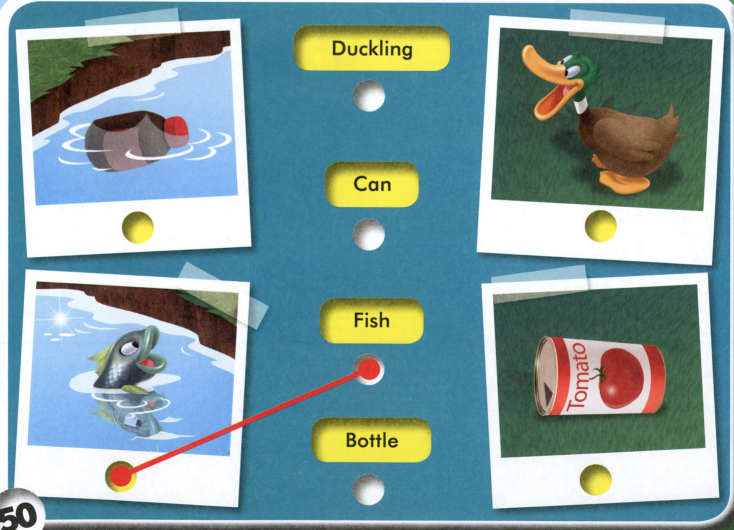

Duckling

Can

Fish

Bottle

50

Moon Mission

?

Goofy's on a mission in space. He'll see the Moon up close! COLOR in the dotted spaces yellow to DISCOVER the three phases of the Moon.

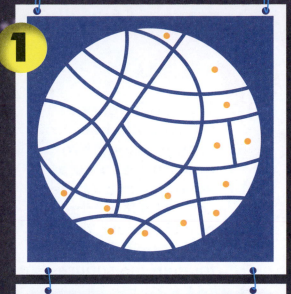

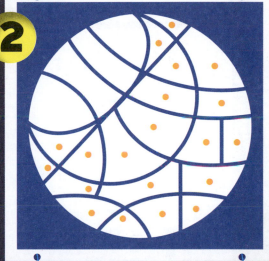

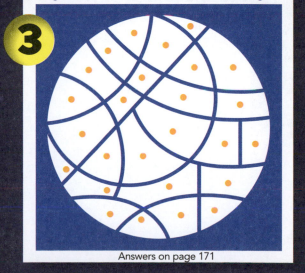

Answers on page 171

It's so Hot!

? The sun is very hot today! Sofia has brought along two accessories to help keep her and Amber cool. LOOK at the objects below, then DRAW and COLOR them in the squares.

ROYAL TABLE SETTING

? Today Sofia is having tea with a friend. Help her learn how to set a table fit for royalty! MATCH the things she needs for the table with the right shadow shapes.

Answers on page 171

SEA CLEAN UP!

? What a disaster! The wind has blown trash from the Jolly Roger into the sea. Quick, help the crew clean it up! TRACE a path from object to object. Then COUNT how many of each type of trash you've collected.

Answers on page 171

LET'S HAVE TEA

? Doc has invited Lambie and Stuffy to have tea. What is missing from the table? CHECK the right objects below!

56

Happy Ears!

? Today Doc is checking her friends' little ears with a special tool. CHECK the one she uses below, then COLOR in Lambie, Stuffy, and Chilly.

Answer on page 171

TRAIN TOGETHER!

? Learning a new sport is fun, especially if Oso teaches you! Shoot some hoops with the Special Agent and then put these three scenes in the right ORDER. COLOR in Oso, too.

DO IT YOURSELF!

? Do you want to learn how to do things on your own? Learn from Oso! MATCH the scenes that go together by adding the right COLOR to the white circles.

Answers on page 171

SUMMER FUN!

? The Clubhouse gang is going on vacation! FOLLOW the summery items to see where the friends are going.

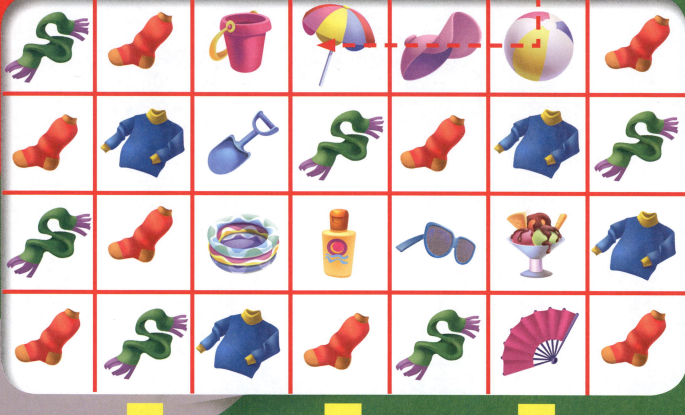

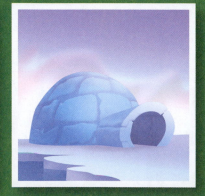

60

Answer on page 171

SPOTLIGHT ON WORDS!

Minnie's photos are in a mess!
Match each picture with the right word.

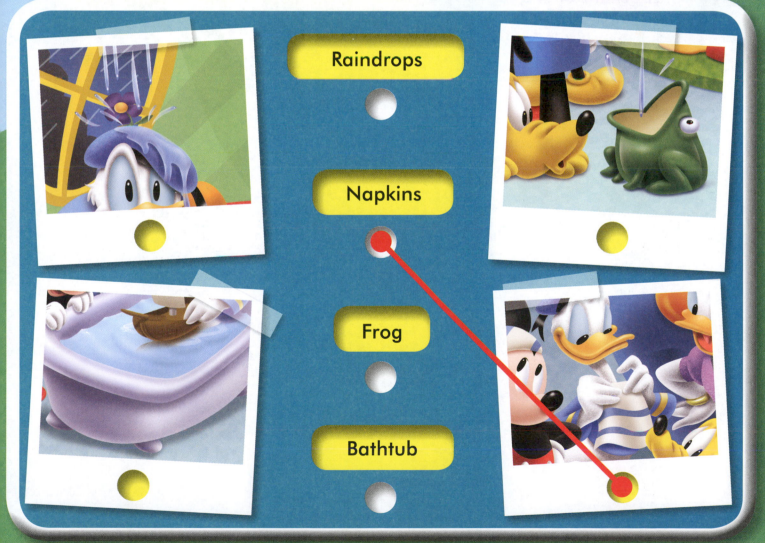

Raindrops

Napkins

Frog

Bathtub

61

DRESSED FOR THE OCCASION

?

The crew is giving a concert and light show in Peter Pan's honor. Can you CHECK Jake's shadow below?

Now join in the fun! FOLLOW the instructions on the next page to MAKE your own pirate hat!

ASK an adult to HELP you TRACE the hat and feather shapes below onto card. Cut out, then GLUE the feather to the hat and add a length of elastic. Now your pirate hat is ready to WEAR!

PARTY LIST!

? Doc is making a list of all the food and decorations for a super party! To help her out, CIRCLE the decorations in pink, and the food for her guests in blue.

Answers on page 17

It's a new day at Doc McStuffins' clinic, and lots of patients are waiting to see her. Time for a checkup!

Read the story and take Doc's tips on hanging out with new friends, plus learn new words.

The doctor is always in!

Today, Doc has found a new toy she really likes. It's a cellphone, and his name's Louie.

"Hello!" Louie yells. But his voice is so loud that Lambie gets scared.

Then Doc hears mom coming. "Your toy is very loud!" mom says, looking at Louie. "It's time for bed." Doc will keep playing tomorrow.

Now Doc is in bed with her toys, and she's ready to sleep.

When mom leaves, the toys come to life and Louie wishes Doc a very loud "Good night".

Next morning Louie yells, waking everybody up. Doc and her toys smile and invite him to play at the clinic.

Louie is very happy to meet Hallie and Chilly, but he speaks too loudly! It's really annoying—he can't help talking so loudly!

Hmm... very strange! Doc wonders if there's something wrong with Louie. She decides to have a look.

Louie is worried about the checkup, but Doc reassures him. Now Louie is ready!

He opens his mouth wide and shouts, "Aaahhh!" Doc holds her ears! Louie certainly has something wrong!

Then, Doc listens to Louie's heart and presses all his buttons. Beep, beep, beep!

Doc has her diagnosis: there's something wrong with Louie's volume button.

Yes, the button is stuck by a sticker! Doc gets her tweezers and then pulls it out.

Now Louie can talk in a soft voice. Hurray! The volume button is working again!

Doc and her friends are so happy. "Louie feels much better now!"

Now Louie can sing along with his new friends. He is really enjoying himself!

Everyone wants to talk and play with him. It's so funny holding a speaking cellphone!

"Louie needs a cuddle!" decides Lambie before cuddling him tight. The toys have found a new friend! Lambie gives Louie a cuddle every time they start a new game!

71

A TASTY SALAD!

Answer on page 172

?

A salad is a fresh and tasty meal! FOLLOW the sequence below to choose the ingredients for Manny's salad.

USE this sequence as your guide.

YUM!

SPINNING WHEELS

Answers on page 172

Can you say the Spanish word for wheel?
rueda = rroo-EH-dah

?

Manny's fixed the wheels on all of the different vehicles in Sheetrock Hills. COLOR the circles to MATCH the wheels.

RUEDA

A New Arrival

1

I WANT THAT EGG!

2

On a sunny day in Never Land,
Hook and Smee are out and about.
They want to steal some treasure,
"There's nothing here," says Hook aloud.

Then Hook spots a golden EGG,
He likes shiny treasures the best!
So he quickly climbs up the tree,
And steals the EGG from the nest.

3

4

While Jake and the pirates are playing,
Two birds arrive with something to say.
They tweet they've lost their EGG,
Jake says, "We'll help right away."

The pirates set off on a search,
Jake knows just what to do.
"Someone's stolen the golden EGG,
No prizes for guessing who!"

74

? Can you SPOT these details in the pictures?

5

Hook and Smee are heading home,
Going through Pea Pod Pass.
Hook accidentally drops the EGG,
Which falls down onto the grass.

6

While the pirates are still searching,
Izzy cries, "Look what I see!"
The golden EGG is sitting there,
Hidden underneath a giant pea.

THE EGG IS CRACKING!

7

With the help of Izzy's pixie dust,
The crew places the EGG back.
Suddenly, once in the nest,
The EGG begins to crack!

8

The birds are really happy
To see their baby hatching out.
"We found the EGG just in time!"
Says Jake with a happy shout.

PET-CARE FUN

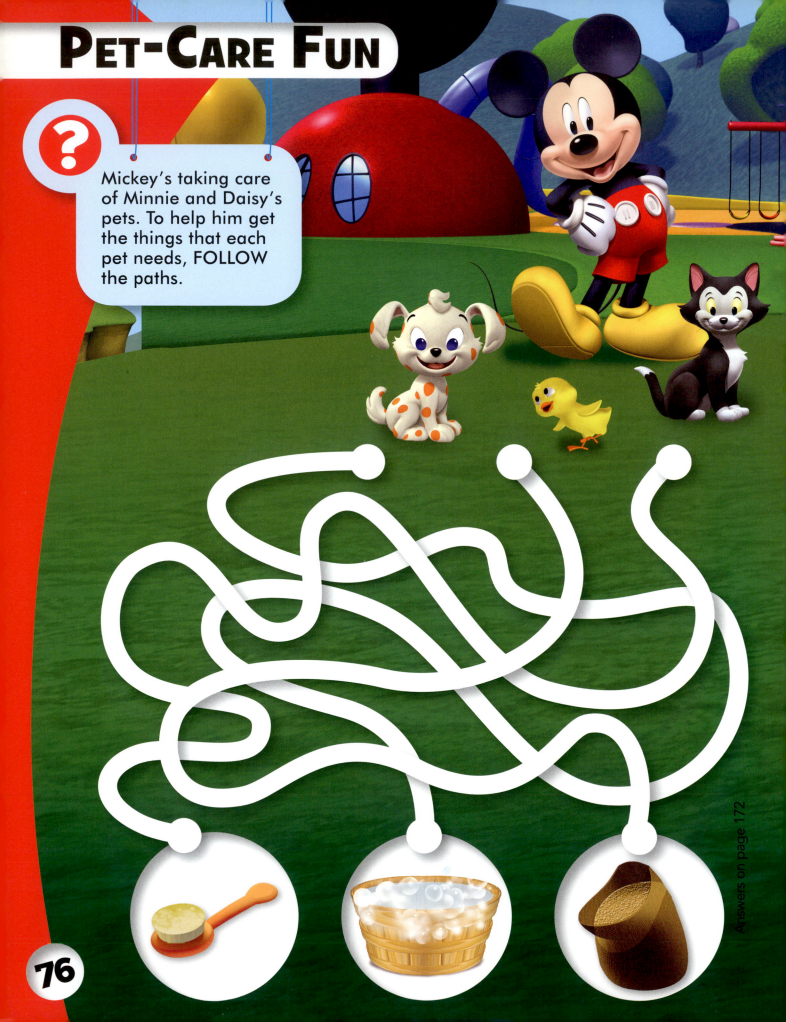

? Mickey's taking care of Minnie and Daisy's pets. To help him get the things that each pet needs, FOLLOW the paths.

Answers on page 172

76

SAME OR DIFFERENT?

Answers on page 172

? Goofy loves to read books all about animals! CHECK the box of the animal that is different in each row.

WORKOUT IN THE PARK

? Today Doc and her pals have gone to the park to enjoy some sports! FOLLOW this workout route with them. When you get to a sign, COPY the exercise shown. TRACE the numbers as you go.

6 TIMES

3 TIMES

START

78

4 TIMES

7 TIMES

FINISH

5 TIMES

Answer on page 172

79

HEALTHY FRUIT DRINK

Hook always loves to rustle up a healthy fruit drink at sunset. Which ingredients does he need? CHECK the right ones, and be careful of the wrong ones!

Answers on page 172

THE FINAL!

?

Jake and Izzy are in the hula hoop finals! It's important to have two trophies in case of a tie. To COMPLETE the second trophy, COPY the squares. Then COLOR in both.

EMERGENCY ON ICE

?

Oh no, a toy has slipped on the ice and can't get back up! What is Doc going to wear to rescue him? To find out, COLOR in the picture and then TRACE the word.

ICE SKATES

NATURE LESSONS

? Doc is showing Stuffy how to recognize plants so that he can take better care of them. Trees, bushes, and flowers all come in different sizes. Help Stuffy by putting them in ORDER, from the smallest to the biggest.

1 ... ... 4 ...

... ... 4

... 1 ... ...

MISSION: HELP THE FISH!

Oso is on another mission—to help Wolfie clean up the seabed so that the fish have a clean place to swim. Join the Special Agent and SPOT the five differences in the second picture!

Answers on page 172

FLYING COLORS

? Oso is set to take off on a mission. There are lots of friends who want to tag along! CIRCLE the matching pairs.

Answers on page 172

UP IN THE SKY!

?

It's a beautiful day— the perfect weather for a hot-air balloon trip! MATCH each balloon to its shadow.

Answers on page 172

THE WAY BACK

? Oh no, the baby chicks have lost their way! But Daisy and Mickey are bringing them back home on the tractor. To see where they live, FOLLOW the path through the maze.

Answer on page 172

SHOOTING STARS

? Doc is in the backyard with her friends. They are watching shooting stars! To COMPLETE the star-filled scene, MATCH the missing parts to the picture.

TRACE the paths of the shooting stars.

88

Answers on page 172

RETURN BY RAFT

? Hook and Smee have played a trick on Cubby—they've hidden the tools he needs to row the raft! What are they? CHECK the happy face for the right ones and the sad face for the wrong ones.

YES → 🙂

NO → 🙁

Answers on page 172

THE RIGHT VEHICLE

? Jake, Izzy, and Skully are all set for new adventures! MATCH each vehicle to a place that they want to visit.

Answers on page 172

STAY ON TRACK

?

Oso and Wolfie are riding head-to-head in a motorbike race. Join them with your friends. All you need is a die and two tokens. FOLLOW the instructions—the first one to cross the finish line wins the medal!

= **2** →

= **STOP**

11

10

12

13

14

FINISH

START

1

2

LET'S SAVE ENERGY!

? Don't forget to turn off the lights when you don't need them! CHECK the happy face for the right way and the sad face for the wrong way. The rule? Turn on the lights only when you need to!

YES → 🙂

NO → 🙁

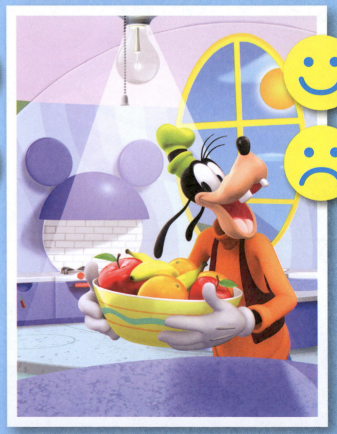

Answers on page 172

A New Dress!

? Minnie is helping Daisy change her old dress into a new dress by adding ribbons and bows. SPOT the five differences in the second picture!

Toys on Wheels

? It's a busy day for Doc, with lots of toys in her clinic waiting for a checkup! CHECK each vehicle as you SPOT it in the scene.

96

Answers on page 172

A Tired Racecar

It's a new day in Doc McStuffins' clinic, and her toy patients are waiting to see her. Time for a checkup!

Read the story, discover Doc's tips for recharging your batteries, and learn new words and phrases.

The doctor is always in!

Today, Doc and Donny are playing with their racecars. Donny's car, Ricardo, is really fast!

Donny is excited! His friend Luca is coming over to play tomorrow. He's sure Ricardo will win!

Three, two, one … the race starts. Ricardo takes the lead right away. One more lap to go and he will win the race!

But suddenly Ricardo slows down and lets the yellow car cross the finish line first.

I'M SORRY!

Oh no! Donny is very disappointed because Ricardo lost the race. He can't believe it!

IT'S NOT FAIR!

CHEER UP, DONNY!

Inside the house, Dad hears Donny crying. So he comes out and tries to cheer him up.

Doc also wants to cheer Donny up. His racecar Ricardo is not very well, and she will try to fix him.

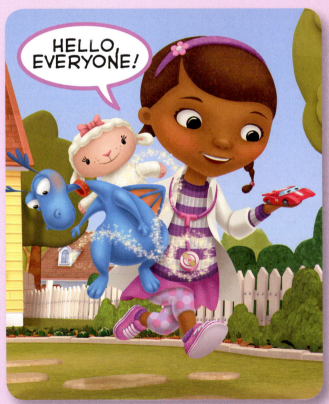

Doc's stethoscope glows, and her toys come to life. It's time to get to work!

Stuffy is really happy to see Ricardo. Ricardo is happy too, but he wonders what's wrong with him.

Doc wants to check what's wrong with Ricardo. So she asks him to race.

But poor Ricardo sputters and stops. He is really worried now. "I have a big race today!"

Doc takes Ricardo to the clinic and gives him a checkup. She lifts his hood and looks at his engine, but everything looks okay.

Hallie knows what is going on. "He looks worn out!" she says. "Yes! He raced too many times last night!" Doc agrees.

"I am feeling a bit tired!" Ricardo says. Doc reassures him. Now she has a diagnosis!

Yes! Ricardo needs to recharge his battery. He is suffering from "No-vroom-vroom-atosis!"

Doc takes Ricardo back to Donny's room and asks Dad to plug Ricardo into the charger.

When Luca comes over, Ricardo's battery is charged and he is ready to race!

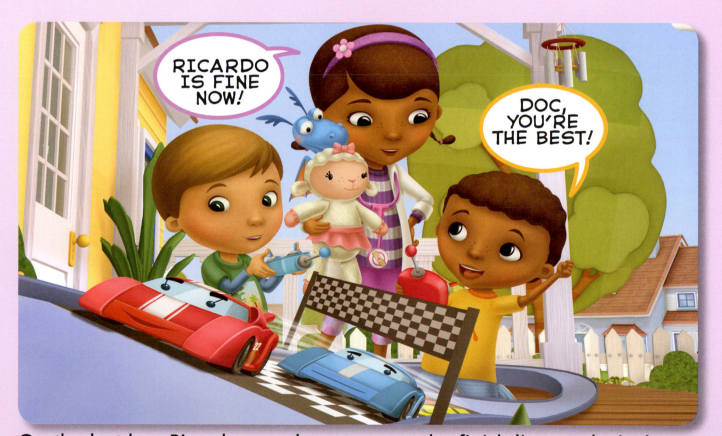

On the last lap, Ricardo speeds up, crosses the finish line, and wins! Donny is so happy. His sister is the best in the world!

MOUNTAINTOP PIRATES!

? Hey, mateys, it's the final stretch to the top of the mountain! Izzy's already there, and Jake and Cubby are on their way. CHECK the climbing equipment among the objects and FOLLOW the pirates through the snow maze.

104

Answers on page 172

105

THE RIGHT BINS!

Mickey, Pluto, and Donald want to throw out the things they don't need anymore. Plastic, paper, and glass must be placed in separate containers. FOLLOW the paths to help them find the right recycling bins.

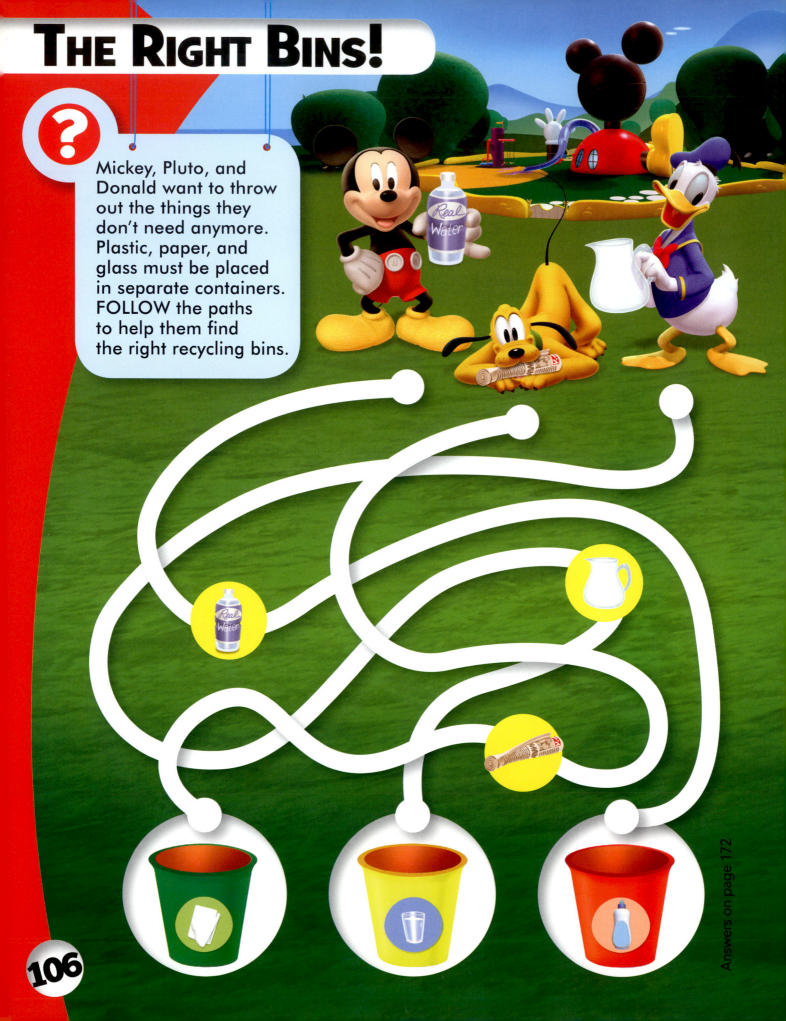

Answers on page 172

THE COLORS OF THE RAINBOW

Mickey and his friends are ready for a new Clubhouse adventure!

Read the story, discover the wonders of the rainbow, and learn new words and phrases.

Come and join the fun!

Read About Rainbows

107

Minnie shows her friends a book about rainbows.

A **RAINBOW** IS AN ARCH OF **LIGHT!**

Minnie tells her friends that a rainbow has many colors.

LOOK AT THESE **COLORS!**

I CAN'T **COUNT** THEM!

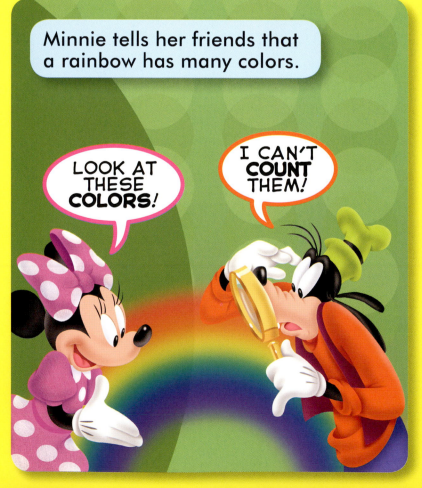

But here are the six that we can see most clearly!

RED, ORANGE, YELLOW, GREEN, BLUE, AND VIOLET!

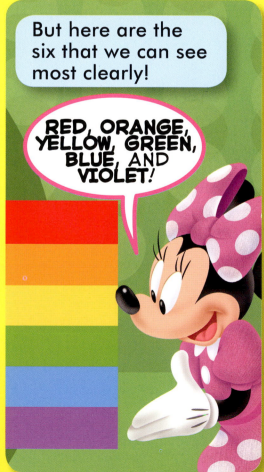

So Minnie has an idea. They will all play the rainbow game!

LET'S LOOK FOR THE **COLORS** OF THE **RAINBOW!**

GREAT IDEA!

In the garden, Mickey finds something red.

LOOK! **STRAWBERRIES** ARE RED!

RED IS THE **FIRST COLOR** OF THE **RAINBOW!**

Goofy is driving his orange car.

ORANGE IS THE **SECOND COLOR** OF THE **RAINBOW!**

Near the pond, Pluto finds some yellow ducklings.

YELLOW IS THE **THIRD COLOR** OF THE **RAINBOW!**

Minnie spots some green things in the vegetable garden.

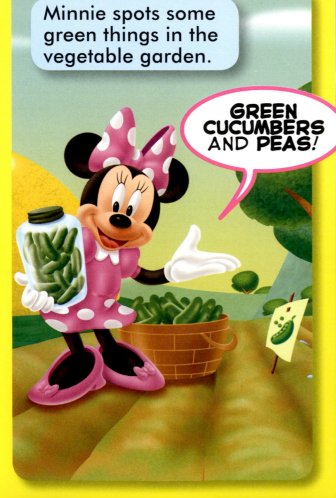

GREEN CUCUMBERS AND **PEAS!**

Here's Donald, on his blue deckchair!

BLUE IS THE RAINBOW'S FIFTH COLOR!

THE END

ANIMAL HEIGHTS

Answers on page 172

? Doc wants to learn all about her animal pals, so she is measuring their heights. Help her by putting them in ORDER, from the shortest to the tallest.

Can you SPOT Doc's mom in the scene?

112

1

CUDDLES FOR FRIENDS

? Doc's toy friends are lining up to have a cuddle with her! Who is late for a cuddle? To find out, TRACE the outline, then add COLOR.

113

Answer on page 172

GREAT OUTDOURS!

? Like all dogs, Pluto loves being outdoors! To make his afternoon even more fun, COLOR in this scene—USE the color of the outlines to help you.

114

ALL ABOUT ANIMALS

Answers on page 172

? Mickey is learning new things about farm animals, like who makes honey, and who gives us wool and milk. To COMPLETE the sequences, DRAW the missing things.

Make Music!

?

Doc uses things she already has at home to create new games. You can do the same—FOLLOW these steps to MAKE wind chimes that play in the breeze!

!

ASK an adult to HELP you.

1 You'll need: 6 yogurt cups; 7 strands of yarn; 6 bottle tops; colored paper; 1 paper plate; safety scissors; glue; tape.

2 Make a hole in the bottom of each cup. Thread the yarn through, then tape a bottle top to the yarn inside.

3 Cut out different shapes from colored paper and glue them onto the cups.

4 Make 7 holes in the paper plate and tie on the yarns. Then tie another yarn to the center, and hang up your chimes.

PIRATE RACE

?

Izzy and Cubby are about to set out on this obstacle course. Going forward and backward, they pick up real pirate objects. To become part of the crew, play with a friend. Take turns to ROLL the die and MOVE the number of spaces shown. CHECK the objects you land on. The first player to check them all, wins!

GO FORWARD 2 SPACES!

3

1 2

START

18 FINISH 17 16

PLAYER 1

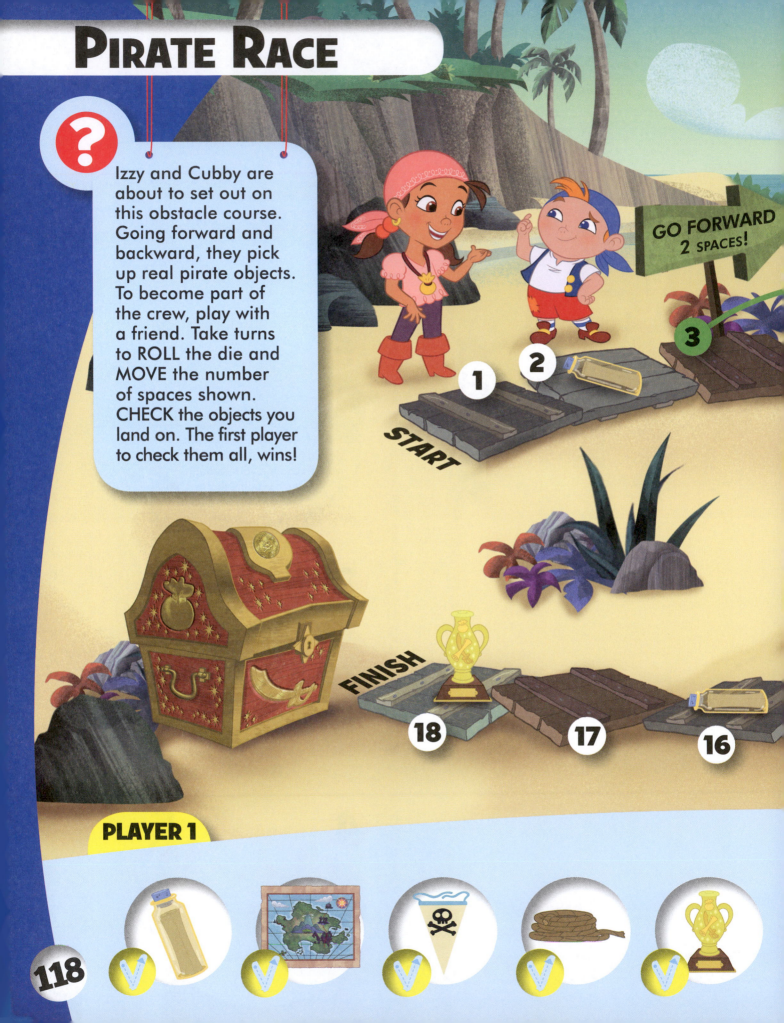

FLOWERS FOR MOM

?

Sofia is collecting flowers for her mom. With a friend, take turns to ROLL a die and FOLLOW the signs and arrows as you MOVE around the path. If you land on a flower space, COLOR one on your scoreboard. The first player to COLOR in all of their flowers, wins!

16

1

15

14

13

STOP!
LOSE 1 TURN

12

11

10

PLAYER 1

A Sandy Ship!

? A gust of wind has turned the Jolly Roger into a beach! Smee needs to get rid of the sand. MATCH the shadows to the objects he needs to do the job.

Answers on page 173

OVER THE SNOW

Answer on page 173

Cubby and Izzy have decided to take a trip to Ice Cube Canyon. Which vehicle will they use there? FOLLOW the S trail to find out!

T	T	S	P	R	H
S	S	S	N	R	K
S	C	R	H	L	D
S	S	S	S	S	Z
V	V	M	R	S	F

123

HELP BABY BIRD!

?

Sofia has found a baby bird that has fallen from its nest. She wants to help him! Put these three scenes in the right ORDER to lead him back home.

COLOR the notes that the mommy bird sings to call the baby bird.

Answer on page 173

125

THE CLEAN-UP GAME!

Doc and her friends are going to play the clean-up game and put their toys in the wagon. With a friend, take turns to ROLL a die and MOVE along the path. If you land on a space with an object, CHECK it below. As you go, COUNT the scraps of paper that need to be collected from the ground. The winner is the player who picks up the most objects!

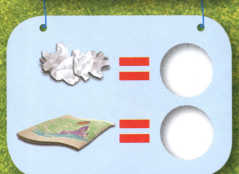

START

1
2
3
4
5
6
7
8

PLAYER 1

A Colorful Mural

Manny and Kelly are painting a mural. It's fun to mix colors and make new ones! COLOR in the white spaces where the circles overlap. Use the color of the outlines to help you.

Can you say the Spanish word for brush? *brocha* = BRO-CHA

BROCHA

Answers on page 173

128

CREEPY CRAWLY SHADOWS

?

On a trip to the park, Kelly has brought along a book about insects. To help Manny get to know them better, MATCH each insect to its shadow.

A Great Nose

1

The sun was out in Jungle Junction,
It was a lovely, cheerful day.
Bobby was patrolling the High Road,
To make sure everything was okay.

2

Suddenly, Bobby spotted some smoke,
It was rising high up in the air.
"I wonder what it is," he said,
"I'd better get over there."

3

On his way, Bobby met Crocker,
He had seen the rising smoke, too.
Crocker had his fire hose ready,
He knew what he had to do.

IT'S A FIRE!

4

The friends followed the smoke,
And came across a burning FIRE.
They needed to put it out quickly,
Before the flames got any higher.

130

? ORDER the fire hoses, from the smallest to the biggest.

5

Just then, Ellyvan arrived to help,
They needed some water, fast!
Crocker gave him the hose to fill,
So they could give the FIRE a blast.

6

Ellyvan went down to the lake,
But the hose pipe was too short.
How could Ellyvan get water?
The elephant thought and thought.

7

Suddenly, Ellyvan had an idea,
He put his trunk in the lake,
And sucked up lots of water,
As much as his trunk could take.

8

Then he rushed back to the others,
And quickly put the FIRE out.
"Ellyvan has saved the day!"
Said Crocker with a shout.

Answer on page 173

SNOWY SCENE

?

Doc's backyard looks so different after it snows. Her friends are enjoying a snowball fight! To COMPLETE this wintry scene, MATCH the puzzle pieces to the picture.

CHECK the vehicle they need to race over the snow!

Answers on page 173

133

SHARING THE SLIDE

I WANT TO GO ON THE SLIDE!

1

Chen and Ada were at the playground,
And something was wrong.
They both wanted to ride the **SLIDE**,
And there was only room for one.

2

Agent Oso was far away,
On a mountain learning to ski,
When a special alert came through;
"Chen and Ada need me!"

3

Oso didn't waste any time,
He arrived at lightning speed.
"I'm here to help," he told his friends,
"I heard you were in need."

4

Paw Pilot told them what to do,
"There are three special steps to learn,
Agent Oso will teach them to you,
Then you can each take a turn."

Having fun at the playground? CHECK the wrong object!

"Step one is very easy,
You have something to decide.
You must choose which person
Will be the first to use the SLIDE."

"I'll go first," said Ada.
Now they were ready for step two.
Ada had to go down the SLIDE.
"I know what I have to do!"

"Well done!" said Agent Oso.
"Now listen carefully.
It's Chen's turn to use the SLIDE,
Then you've completed step three."

Later, back on the mountain,
Oso cried out, "Look at me!"
He was sledding through the snow.
"It's easier to SLIDE than ski!"

Answer on page 173

Country Race

?

It's race day at the Clubhouse! TRACE each path, then COUNT the number of fences Minnie's pony has jumped over. Then count the number of balls Daisy's bunny has jumped over.

136

Sofia's Dance Lesson

1

Sofia's mom has a special surprise.
"We're holding a ball for you!"
But poor Sofia can't dance,
She doesn't know what to do.

I LOVE THESE SHOES!

2

Sofia's stepsister, Amber,
Gives her dancing SHOES to try.
"She must finally like me!"
Says Sofia with a sigh.

3

But when Sofia wears the SHOES,
They just make her fall down!
"Amber has put a spell on them!"
Sofia says with a frown.

4

So Sofia visits Cedric, the sorcerer.
He teaches her a magic spell.
When she says the magic words,
She'll be able to dance really well.

? Can you SPOT these details in the pictures?

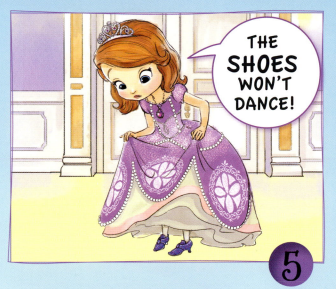

Sofia looks at her SHOES,
It's almost time for the ball.
She's ready to try to dance!
She hopes she doesn't fall.

But when the magic words are said,
Everyone falls asleep.
Sofia's brother, mom, and dad,
Even Cedric's in a deep sleep.

"Please give me another chance!"
Says Amber, sorry for her mistake.
Then she teaches Sofia to dance.
And with a new spell the guests awake.

And the ball is truly magical,
Sofia dances with success.
Every step is perfect,
She feels like a true princess!

Answers on page 173

FIXING FEET

1

The Tools were having fun playing,
When Manny received a call.
It was Francisco at the ranch,
He needed the help of them all.

2

They arrived as quickly as they could,
Francisco greeted them happily.
"Thanks for coming, y'all.
You're such good friends to me."

GREAT HORSE!

3

The Tools spotted Francisco's HORSE
Standing quietly in the sun.
"I wish we were cowboys!" Turner said,
"That would be so much fun!"

4

The HORSE was looking very sad,
She had broken her horseshoe.
"She can't walk," Francisco said,
"Is there something you can do?"

140

Put the cowboy
hats in ORDER,
from the smallest
to the biggest!

Manny and Pat made a start,
There was no time to waste.
They worked together as a team,
To fix the HORSE's shoe with haste.

Now the HORSE could walk again,
She trotted off with delight.
She kicked her legs with glee,
It was such a happy sight!

Francisco was very pleased,
He had a special treat in store.
He let the Tools ride the HORSE,
They couldn't have asked for more!

"Now we're genuine cowboys!"
Turner shouted out with glee.
"Giddy up, HORSE!" he cried,
As the Tools cheered happily.

4   1

Answer on page 173

141

SPOTLIGHT ON WORDS!

Goofy's photos are in a mess!
Match each picture with the right word.

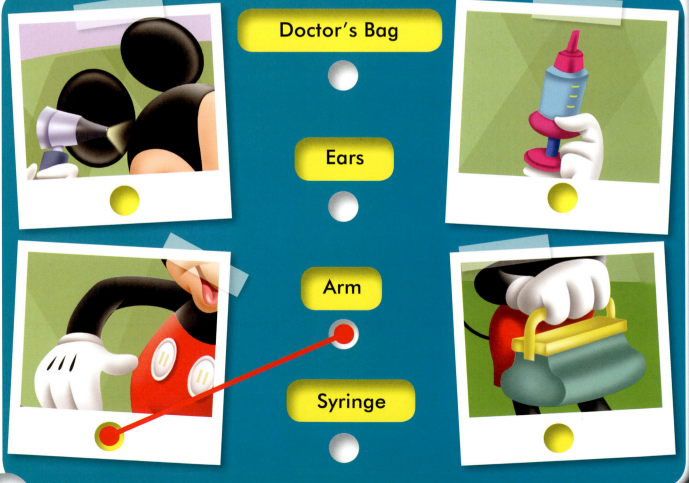

Doctor's Bag

Ears

Arm

Syringe

142

Answers on page 173

FLOWER POWER!

Minnie's taking pictures of pretty flowers. SPOT the five differences in the second picture.

Answers on page 173

143

LIKE NEW!

? Doc loves to fix Donny's broken toys instead of throwing them out. Put these three scenes in the right ORDER.

144

Answer on page 173

WATERY FUN

? The fountain in Doc's backyard has sprung a leak! It needs to be fixed right away—water is being wasted! Doc is using some objects to collect the water. To find out what they are, COLOR in the dots in the pictures below.

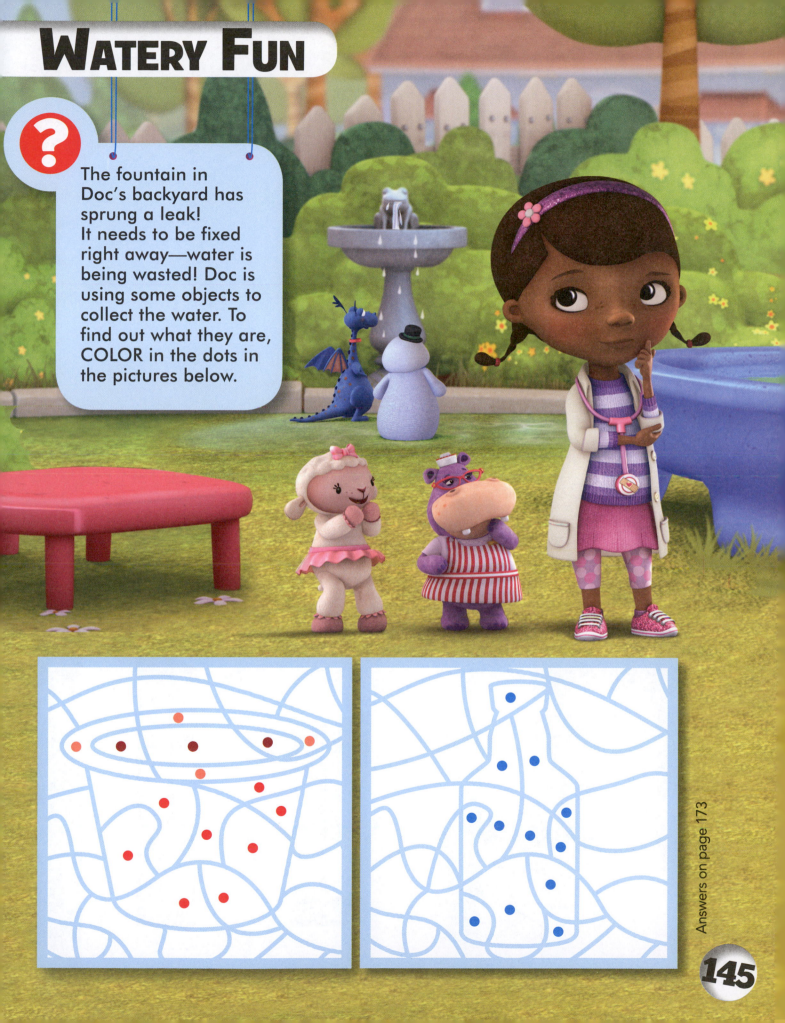

Answers on page 173

145

FLYING FREE!

? Mia is flying by Sofia's window. Sofia dreams of flying, too! CONNECT the dots and then COLOR in the sweet songbird.

COLLECTING CONES

? While walking in the woods, Sofia has found some pine cones. She's learned to make some pretty things with them! CHECK the pictures below that show her pine cone creations.

Answers on page 173

147

ON THE MOVE

The search is on for the puzzle box! Peter Pan has already spotted it. To COMPLETE the scene, MATCH the missing parts to the picture.

Can you SPOT the puzzle box hidden in the scene?

Answers on page 173

THE GET-TO-THE-BARN GAME!

? It's naptime, and the pig and the lamb must hurry to the barn. With a friend, take turns to ROLL the die and MOVE along the path. The first player to reach the barn, wins!

START

1

2

3

4

5

10

11

12

GO FORWARD 2 SPACES

GO FORWARD 2 SPACES

LOSE YOUR NEXT TURN!

SHARE WITH SMEE!

? Hook's not around, so Smee is celebrating with a fruit cake! He's invited Jake and his crew to share it. Can you MATCH the cake slices to the whole cake?

152

Answers on page 173

SAFE SKATER

? It's time for some skateboard tricks! Izzy should wear something that protects her if she falls. Peter Pan knows what it is. Do you? CHECK the right object!

153

Answer on page 173

SHADOW STEPS!

Answer on page 173

?

Sofia is learning to dance like a princess! In the light, Sofia casts a shadow on the floor. SPOT the right one and CHECK it.

154

WOODLAND WALK

After school, Sofia enjoys a walk in the woods with her bird friends. One of them has lost a feather. FIND the feather and CHECK the bird it belongs to.

Answer on page 173

155

RIPE STRAWBERRIES!

It's time for Doc to pick some strawberries to have as a healthy and delicious snack. COUNT the red strawberries, as well as the yellow and the blue flowers.

1 2 3 4 5

TAILWIND!

? Some playful dolphins have swiped an object from each Never Land pirate raft! Luckily, a tailwind will help the crews catch up with them. FOLLOW the paths to see what our friends have lost.

Real pirates must always know which way the wind is blowing. COLOR the compass in one direction only.

NORTH

WEST

EAST

SOUTH

FUNNY FRIENDS

? Today, two funny little friends have brought smiles to Doc's clinic! Put these three scenes in the right ORDER.

Answer on page 173

MAKING MUSIC

? Doc's brother, Donny, and his friend Emmie want to give a concert. But where are the xylophone sticks? FOLLOW the maze to help Doc find them.

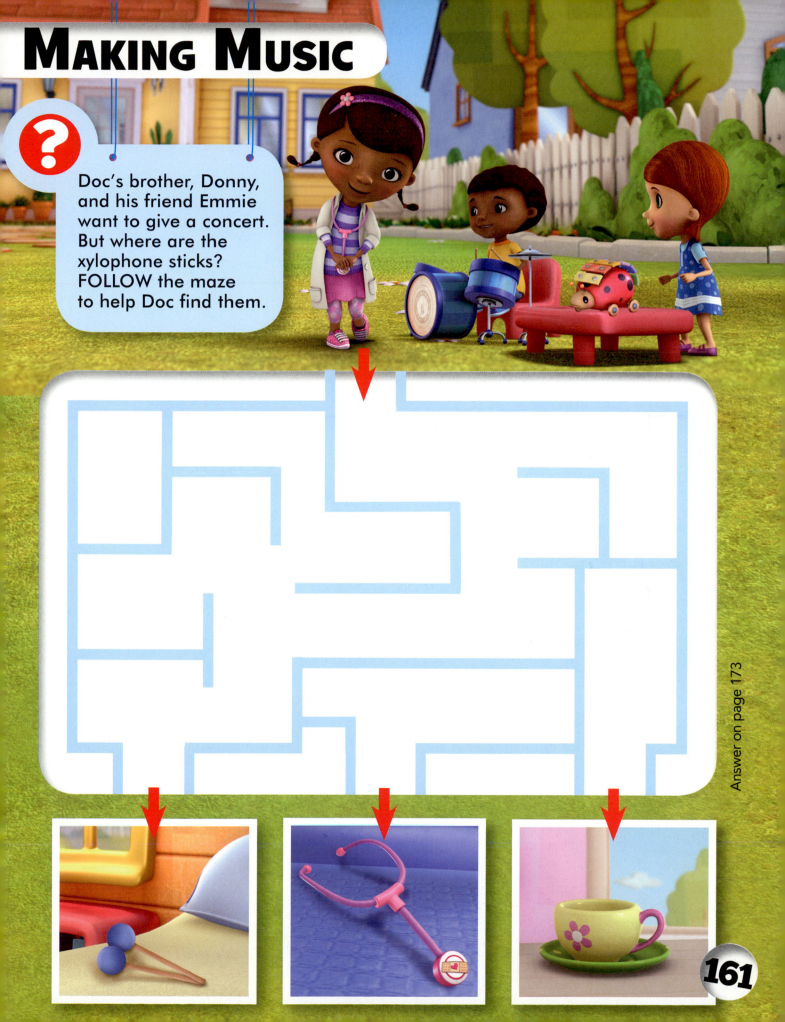

Answer on page 173

161

ROYAL BUFFET

? Sofia is learning the difference between finger food and dishes that require knives and forks. Use the guide below to COLOR in the dots correctly.

Answers on page 173

A Bright Night

WE'RE MAKING PRESENTS!

1

Kelly was having a Christmas party,
It was going to be lots of fun.
The Tools were making PRESENTS.
Felipe said, "We're almost done."

2

Just then Mayor Rosa called,
The lights on the town tree were out.
"The carol singing is starting soon!"
Said Mayor Rosa with a shout.

3

Manny and the Tools arrived
And fixed the lights without delay.
They were ready in time for the carols,
And soon the singing was underway.

4

While going to Kelly's party,
Manny spotted someone else in need.
Mrs. Portillo had lost her key,
She was very worried indeed.

Can you SPOT these details in the pictures?

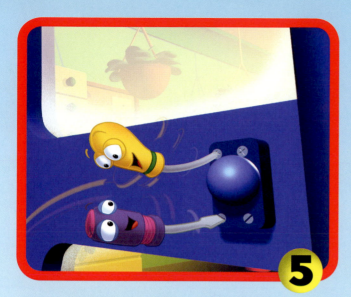

5

"We'll help you, Mrs. Portillo!"
Turner and Felipe cried.
They unscrewed the doorknob
So that she could get inside.

6

Soon they were on their way again,
But they didn't get very far.
Sherman was stuck in the snow,
And needed help to push his car.

7

Manny and the Tools missed the party,
They had to go back home instead.
Without exchanging PRESENTS,
They all headed sadly to bed.

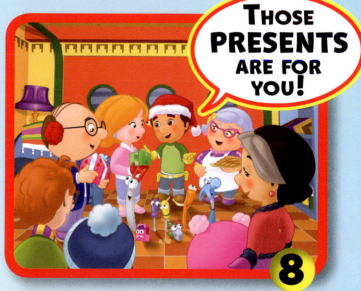

THOSE **PRESENTS** ARE FOR YOU!

8

But Kelly had brought the party there,
The Tools couldn't believe their eyes!
They handed out their PRESENTS
And said, "Thank you for the surprise!"

Answers on page 173

HOOK'S HAPPY CREW!

?

Today Hook's crew is going to celebrate their friendship and all of their great adventures together! What gifts have they got? To find out, COLOR the white circles to match each gift with its package. Then TRACE the name of this pirate holiday.

CREW'S DAY

167

Answers on page 173

RAIN OR SHINE!

Answers on page 173

Doc knows the secret to staying well, whatever the weather! You just have to choose the right accessory to protect yourself from the sun and the rain. MATCH each accessory to the right weather.

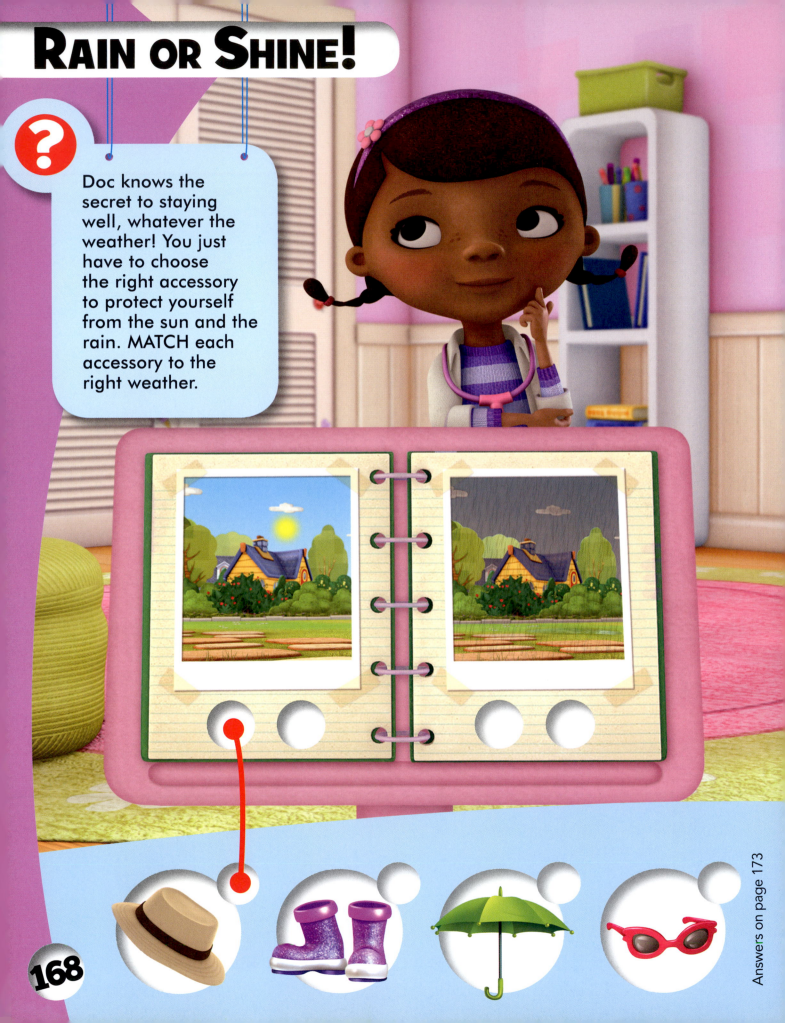

PALS IN THE POOL

?

Doc and her friends are having some fun in the backyard swimming pool. SPOT the five differences in the second picture.

Answers on page 173

169

MEAL FOR TWO!

? Donald and Mickey have ordered a tasty dish to share at the restaurant. FOLLOW the path to find out what it is.

Answer on page 173

ANSWERS

Page 6–7

Page 8

Page 9

Page 10–11

Page 14–15

Page 16

Page 17

Page 18–19

Page 20–21

Page 22
The purple cupcake is Stuffy's, the orange cupcake is the crab's and the pink cupcake is Doc's.

Page 23

Page 26

Page 27

Page 28–29

Page 30

Page 31

Page 32
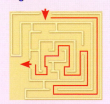

Page 33

Page 34–35

Page 36–37

Page 40–41

Page 42

Page 43
VEGETABLE SOUP

Page 44–45

Page 46

Page 47

Page 48

Page 49

Page 50

Page 51

Page 53

Page 54–55

Page 56

Page 57

Page 58

Page 59

Page 60

ANSWERS

Page 61

Page 62–63

Page 64

Page 72

Page 73

Page 74–75

Page 76
The dog needs the bubble bath, the chick needs the grain and the cat needs the brush.

Page 77

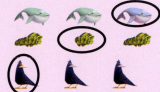

Page 78–79

Page 80

Page 83

Page 84

Page 85

Page 86

Page 87

Page 88–89

Page 90

Page 91

Page 94

Page 95

Page 96

Page 104–105

Page 106
Mickey will use the red bin, Pluto will use the green bin and Donald will use the yellow bin.

Page 112

Page 113
Squeakers

Page 115

Page 122

Page 123

Page 124–125

Page 128

Page 129

Page 130–131

Page 132–133

Page 134–135

Page 136–137

Minnie's pony jumped three times and Daisy's bunny jumped four times.

Page 138–139

Page 140–141

Page 142

Page 143

Page 144

Page 145

A bucket and a bottle.

Page 147

Page 148–149

Page 152   **Page 153**

Page 154   **Page 155**

Page 156–157

Page 158–159
Jake and Cubby have lost Jake's sword, the pirates have lost a rubber ring and Hook and Smee have lost Hook's boot.

Page 160

Page 161

Page 162–163

Page 164–165

Page 166–167

Page 168

Page 169

Page 170